Pixie Tricks

The Greedy
Gremlin

Catch all of the Pixie Tricks adventures!

Sprite's Secret

• • •

The Greedy Gremlin

PIXIE TRICKS

The Greedy Gremlin

· by ·
TRACEY WEST

—— A ——
LITTLE APPLE
PAPERBACK
————————

SCHOLASTIC INC.
New York Toronto London Auckland Sydney
Mexico City New Delhi Hong Kong

Book design by Dawn Adelman

ISBN 0-439-17219-5

Cover and sticker illustrations by James Bernardin
Interior illustrations by Thea Kliros

All rights reserved. Published by Scholastic Inc., 555 Broadway, New York, NY 10012, by arrangement with Scholastic Inc. SCHOLASTIC and associated logos are trademarks and/or registered trademarks of Scholastic Inc.

12 11   4 5/0

Printed in the U.S.A.   40
First Scholastic printing, May 2000

For Terry West, who could
teach Jolt a thing or two
about playing video games.

— T. W.

·· Contents ··

Fourteen pixies have escaped;

They're causing so much trouble.

Sprite and Violet's secret job

Is to trick them on the double!

Pix was tricked the last time.

He loved to play and play.

But Sprite and Violet gave him work

To send him far away.

With thirteen pixies left to trick,

This tale has just begun.

Tricking pixies can be hard —

But it's also lots of fun!

Chapter One
A Pixie Plan

It must have been a dream, Violet Briggs told herself.

Violet crunched on her cereal. She stared out the window. Today seemed like any other day. The sun was shining outside. She was eating breakfast. Safe at her kitchen table.

Today wasn't anything like yesterday. Yesterday she thought she met a fairy. A fairy named Sprite. And she thought she

traveled with magic pixie dust. And saved the world from a pixie named Pix.

"No way," Violet said, shaking her head. "It had to be a dream. It just had to."

Just then, drops of milk splashed in her face.

Violet looked down. A tiny fairy sat on the edge of her cereal bowl.

It was Sprite.

"Could a dream do that?" Sprite asked. He kicked the milk with his tiny boot.

Violet sighed. "I guess not. But I still can't believe you're real."

Sprite flew in front of her face. "I'm real, all right!"

Violet laughed. Sprite's wings tickled her cheeks.

"Okay," Violet said. "You're real. But can

you tell me again what you're doing here? I'm still kind of confused."

Sprite sat back down on the cereal bowl. "Okay. I'm a fairy. I live in the Otherworld. One day, fourteen fairies escaped into your world."

"Through the oak tree in my backyard," Violet said.

"Right," Sprite said. "Then Queen Mab, the fairy queen, came to me. Because I'm a Royal Pixie Tricker."

"And your job is to trick the escaped pixies and send them back to the Otherworld," said Violet.

"Right again," Sprite said. "Just like we tricked Pix."

Sprite reached into a small bag around his waist. He took out a tiny book. It was the *Book of Tricks.*

Sprite flipped through the book. He opened it to a page that said "Pix." There was a picture of the fairy on the page.

Pix showed up right after Violet met Sprite. If Pix tapped you on the head, you would forget about work. And chores. And friends. And family. You would just want to play and play. But Violet and Sprite tricked him. Now Pix was back in the Otherworld.

Violet was glad to see Pix in the *Book of Tricks*. It meant he was there for sure. Before he was tricked, the page was blank.

"I can't believe we tricked Pix," Violet said. "It wasn't easy."

Sprite reached into the cereal bowl. He picked up a round piece of cereal. It was almost as big as his head.

Sprite took a tiny bite of the bright green cereal.

"Not bad," he said. "This almost tastes like fairy food. Is it magic?"

Violet looked at the box of cereal. Beastie Bites. Her favorite.

"No," she said. "But it has eight essential vitamins and minerals."

Sprite munched. "I think we should try to trick another pixie today."

"How about Hinky Pink?" Violet asked.

"Hinky Pink?" Sprite asked.

"You know, that fairy who controls the weather. The one who tried to trap us in the fog yesterday," Violet said. "We could go back to the playground. He might still be there."

"We could," Sprite said. "But it might be dangerous."

"Why?" Violet asked.

"Pixies come in all sizes," Sprite said. "Pix was one of the smaller ones. Like me. But Hinky Pink is different."

"You mean he's big?" Violet asked.

Sprite nodded. "Like a human. Sometimes the big ones are harder to trick. But not always."

"Well, I'm ready this time," Violet said. She pulled her backpack out from under the table. She took out mittens, an umbrella, and sunscreen.

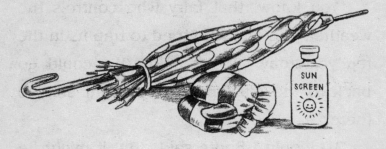

"See? If he changes the weather again, we'll be ready," Violet said.

Sprite seemed impressed. "Not bad," he said. "But why did you do all this? I thought you said it was all a dream."

"Well, like Aunt Anne always says, it's better to be safe than sorry!" Violet answered.

Violet zipped up her backpack. "Let's do it!" she said. "Let's go trick another pixie!"

Chapter Two
Leon

"Violet, what are you doing today?"

Violet jumped at the sound of her mom's voice. She quickly shoved Sprite into her pocket.

Violet's mom came into the kitchen. She had dark brown hair like Violet. She smiled like Violet, too.

"Uh, I'm going to look for something," Violet said.

Violet's mom leaned over and kissed her

on the head. "I'm sorry your dad and I have to work," she said. "Be good for Aunt Anne. And try to get along with Leon."

Violet frowned. Her cousin Leon was not easy to get along with. But they all lived in the same house. So they had to try.

"Okay, Mom," Violet said.

Violet's mom left the room. Sprite popped out of her pocket. He smoothed his rainbow wings.

"Ouch!" he said. "I hate when you do that."

"Sorry," Violet said. "Let's go."

Violet ran down the stairs. She walked through the hall on the first floor, where Leon and Aunt Anne lived.

She started to open the door.

"Hey!" a voice cried. "Stop right there!"

Violet spun around. Sprite hid behind her shoulders.

"What do you want, Leon?" Violet asked.

Leon was dressed in pajama bottoms and a T-shirt. His sandy-blond hair wasn't combed.

"Someone's been messing around with my video game," Leon said. "Was it you?"

"Are you crazy?" Violet said. "I hate video games. You know that."

"It's all messed up. When I want to go up,

I go down. When I want to go right, I go left," Leon said. "If you didn't do it, who did?" He sounded angry.

Violet shrugged. "I don't know. Maybe you played it in your sleep. You play it all the time, anyway."

"Ha-ha," Leon said. He stepped inside his room and slammed the door.

Violet quickly went outside and into the backyard.

"So that was Leon," Sprite said. "I can see why you didn't want him to help us yesterday."

"I told you," Violet said. "He'd spoil everything. Now let's go find Hinky Pink."

"Right," Sprite said. He took his magic bag from his belt. He reached in the bag. He pulled out some pixie dust. The dust would take them wherever they wanted to go.

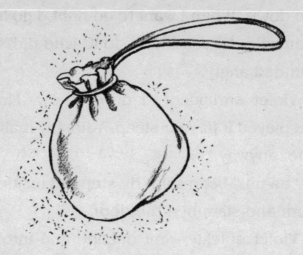

Sprite started to throw the pixie dust.

"Heeeeeeelp!"

Sprite stopped. That voice sounded like Leon.

"He's probably just complaining about his game," Violet said.

"Heeeeeelp!"

"It sounds like he's in trouble," Sprite said.

Violet sighed. "Let's go see."

Violet ran back into the house. Sprite flew behind her. They opened Leon's door.

Violet gasped.

A scary-looking fairy sat on the edge of Leon's bed. The fairy held the controls to the video game system.

And Leon was nowhere in sight!

Chapter Three
Jolt

"Who are you?" Violet asked the fairy. "And where is Leon?"

The fairy ignored her. He kept hitting the buttons on the controls.

Sprite's face lit up. "Jolt! It's you!"

Jolt still didn't reply. Instead, he shouted at the TV screen, "That's it! Almost there! Hee-hee! This is great!"

Jolt was a few inches taller than Sprite. He had a pointy nose. His blue eyes were

streaked with red from staring at the screen. His silvery hair stuck straight up on top of his head.

Sprite flew in front of Jolt's face. He reached into his magic bag and took out a small medal. Violet knew that medal. It said ROYAL PIXIE TRICKER.

Sprite showed the medal to Jolt. "By the order of Queen Mab, I demand that you stop playing this game right now!"

Jolt scowled. He hit the pause button on

the controls. "I'm not stopping because you told me to. I'm stopping because you're in my way! I can't see the screen."

Jolt stood up and glared at Sprite.

Sprite glared back. "Oh, yeah?"

Violet stepped between them. "What did you do with Leon?" she asked Jolt.

Jolt looked at the ceiling. "Leon? I don't know any Leon."

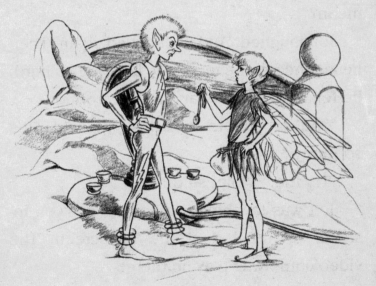

"He's my cousin and this is his room," Violet said. "He was here a minute ago."

"You mean that boy!" Jolt said. His face glowed with excitement. "Oh, yes. Well, I was playing his game, you see. And he started yelling and screaming and making a real fuss. So I took care of him."

Violet was worried. She had seen how fairies take care of things. "What do you mean?"

Jolt laughed. And he laughed again. Then he laughed some more. He laughed so hard, he fell onto the bed and rolled around.

"You're going to love this," he said. "It's so funny."

"Try me," Violet said.

Jolt was laughing too hard to answer. Instead, he pointed at the TV screen. The video game was playing there.

Violet and Sprite looked at the blurry picture paused on the screen.

The words on the bottom of the screen said LEVEL 1. The picture showed a boy running down a mountain. Big rocks were rolling down the mountain, too.

"What are you pointing at?" Violet asked. "Where's Leon?"

Then Violet noticed something. The boy on the screen had messy blond hair. He wore pajama bottoms and a T-shirt.

Violet looked closer.

The boy in the game was Leon!

Chapter Four
Action Kingdom

"Get Leon out of there!" Violet cried.

"Why should I?" Jolt said. "He's a nasty little boy. He's more fun in there."

Jolt hit the play button. The picture on the screen started to move. Leon ran down the mountain as fast as he could. One of the big rocks rolled right behind him.

The rock almost hit Leon. Leon screamed and dodged out of the way.

"This level's too easy," Jolt said. "I can't wait to get to level two."

Violet didn't like video games much. But she knew this one. *Action Kingdom.* Leon played it all the time.

The game had twelve levels. The game's character, Action Andy, had to escape some kind of danger. The danger got bigger with each level.

Leon was already in trouble. And he was only in level one!

"I know Leon's kind of a pain," Violet told Jolt. "But he's my cousin. Can't you please let him out of there?"

"No way!" Jolt said. "I usually just like to mess up video games so people can't play them. But then I started to play Leon's game. It was so much fun! I played all night.

And Leon's even more fun than Action Andy."

Violet turned to Sprite. "Do something!"

"Right," Sprite said. He paused. "Uh, what do *you* think we should do?"

"Not again!" Violet said. "Don't you know how to get Leon out of there?"

"I'm not sure," Sprite said. "Remember, I'm — "

"You're new at this. I know," Violet said. "I guess it's up to me."

Violet reached out. She tried to take the controls from Jolt.

"Ouch!" A tiny electric shock stung her hand.

"Hee-hee," said Jolt. "You can't take this away from me!!!"

"Now what?" Violet asked Sprite.

"Why don't you try to trick me?" Jolt asked. "That's what you're supposed to do, isn't it? Trick me so I'll be sent back home."

"Sprite!" Violet said. "The book!"

Sprite reached into his magic bag. He pulled out the *Book of Tricks.* The book told how to trick every fairy. If the trick worked, the fairy's magic stopped. And the fairy would be sent back to the Otherworld.

Sprite started to open the book. But then Violet stopped him and looked at Jolt.

"Why did you remind us about the trick?" Violet asked Jolt.

"Because it doesn't matter," Jolt said. "Sprite's the worst Pixie Tricker in the Other-world. He failed all of his classes."

Violet stared at Sprite. "You did?"

Sprite blushed. His pale green cheeks turned bright green.

"Not *all* of my classes," he said.

"Well, it doesn't matter," Violet said. "We tricked Pix, right? We can trick Jolt."

"Right," Sprite said. But he didn't sound so sure.

Sprite flipped the pages of the book. "Let me see if it's here. Ah, yes. Here it is. Jolt."

Violet peered at the tiny pages. One page

was blank. The other page had a short rhyme.

"Read the rhyme," Violet said.

Sprite read from the book.

"'Jolt can play all video games,
He has a special knack.
But only if he reads from a book
Will you send him back.'"

"If he reads from a book," Violet repeated. "We've got to get him to read part of a book."

"Hee-hee!" Jolt laughed harder than before. "A book! Imagine that. I've never read a book in my life!"

Violet and Sprite looked at each other.

How could they trick Jolt?

They'd never get him to read a book!

Chapter Five
To the Library!

Inside the game, Leon screamed. He jumped over another rock. He looked like he was too tired to run anymore.

"We've got to do something," Sprite said.

"I have an idea," said Violet.

Jolt laughed again. "Hee-hee! Try your hardest. You'll never trick me," he said. He didn't take his eyes off the video game.

Sprite flew around Violet's face. "Let's

go!" he said. "If you've got a plan, I want to hear it."

Violet looked at the screen. Leon looked miserable. She felt sorry for him.

"I'm afraid to leave," she said. "What if Leon gets hurt in the game?"

"Ha!" Jolt said. "I'm great at this game. I never let Action Andy get hurt."

"Never?" Violet asked.

"Well, almost never," Jolt admitted. "I always lose the game in level eleven."

Violet turned to Sprite. "Then we've got to hurry!" she said.

Violet ran out of the house and into the yard. Sprite flew after her. She stopped at the old oak tree.

"So what's your plan?" Sprite asked.

"I'll tell you," she said. "But first tell me about Jolt. He doesn't look like you. Or Pix."

"Jolt's a gremlin," Sprite said. "They love to mess things up. Especially machines and gadgets."

"What do you mean?" Violet asked.

"Like when your alarm clock doesn't go off and makes you late," Sprite said. "And your computer crashes. And your car won't start. Gremlins do things like that."

"Maybe that's why Leon's video game didn't work right this morning," Violet said.

"Right!" said Sprite. "You heard Jolt. He said he usually likes to mess up games. But now he likes to play them."

"With real people inside." Violet shuddered.

"Is that enough about Jolt?" Sprite asked.

"That's enough about Jolt," Violet said. "But not about you."

Sprite sat on Violet's shoulder. "Here we go again," he said. Violet was always full of questions.

"If you failed all of your Pixie Tricking classes, why did the queen send you here?"

Sprite blushed again. "I'm not sure," he said. "Unless — "

"Unless what?" Violet asked.

"Unless it has something to do with the poem," Sprite said. "Queen Mab read me a poem before she sent me here."

Violet was excited. "How did it go?"

Sprite's wings twitched. "I can't remember it all."

"Try!" Violet said. "It could be important."

"I do remember some of it," Sprite said. "Something like,

'Find a Pixie Tricker,
The youngest in the land.
Send him to the human world,
The Book of Tricks in hand.' "

"I am the youngest Pixie Tricker in the land," Sprite said. "That must be why the queen sent me."

"Okay!" Violet said. "How does the rest go?"

"I really can't remember," Sprite said. "Can't it wait? We have to help Leon."

"You're right," Violet said. "I think I know what to do. We need to go to the library."

"No problem," Sprite said. He reached into his bag. He took out more pixie dust.

Violet took a deep breath. Traveling with pixie dust always made her a little dizzy. It made her sneeze, too.

Violet held her nose. "I'm ready!" she said. Sprite sprinkled the pixie dust over their heads.

"To the library!" Sprite cried.

Chapter Six
Books for Jolt

Violet's skin tingled. The oak tree vanished.

A light flashed in front of her eyes. She blinked. She opened her eyes.

She wasn't in the yard anymore.

But she wasn't in the library, either.

She was in the mall!

"Not again!" she said. Yesterday, Sprite had landed them in the mall by mistake, too.

"Sorry," Sprite said. He took out some more pixie dust.

Violet stopped him. "Wait," she said. "Look over there."

Violet and Sprite were in front of a video game store. A group of boys and girls were inside the store. Each kid held video game controls.

"My controls don't work anymore!" one girl complained.

"Mine, too," said a boy. "When I want to go up, I go down. When I want to go left, I go right."

Violet gasped. "That's what happened to Leon's controls."

Sprite looked worried. "This is worse than I thought. Jolt has been messing up video games all over town. When he's done with Leon, he might trap these kids in their video games, too."

"We've got to hurry!" Violet said.

"Right!" said Sprite. He threw the pixie dust again.

Violet closed her eyes. She held her nose.

When she opened her eyes, she was in the library.

Sitting on top of a tall bookshelf!

Sprite was hiding behind a book. He slowly peeked his head out.

"Sprite," Violet moaned. "Can't you get it right just once?"

Sprite popped out and shrugged. "Landing is the hardest part. We can climb down."

"Violet Briggs! What are you doing up there?"

Sprite ducked behind the book. Violet

looked down. It was Ms. Bowley, the librarian.

"Uh," Violet said.

"Cleaning the ceiling?" Sprite told Violet in a whisper.

"No!" Violet said. The librarian looked at her strangely.

"I mean, I was trying to reach a book," Violet said. "And I kind of got stuck."

"Violet, I'm surprised at you. You know better than that," the librarian said.

"Sorry," Violet said. "I, um, just need to get some books. It's really important."

Ms. Bowley sighed. "Well, then you should have asked for some help." She picked up a stepladder and set it below Violet. "Here. Climb down," she said.

"Thank you," Violet said. She climbed down from the shelf.

"Now, how can I help you?" Ms. Bowley asked.

Violet thought. She really couldn't tell Ms. Bowley about Jolt. But maybe the librarian could still help.

"I need to find a book for somebody who doesn't like to read," Violet said.

Curious, Sprite flew closer. He hid behind another book.

"What does this person like?" Ms. Bowley asked.

"Machines. And gadgets," Sprite whispered softly.

"He likes machines and gadgets," Violet told Ms. Bowley.

"Hmmm," she replied. "Anything else?"

"Video games," Violet said. "Especially *Action Kingdom*."

The librarian walked to a shelf. "I have a few books your friend might like." She began to take books and hand them to Violet.

"Here's *The Wonderful Wizard of Oz*," she said. "And *Peter Pan*. And *Treasure Island*. These books have lots of action and adventure. They're better than video games, if you ask me."

Violet put the books on the librarian's

desk. She took her library card from her sweater pocket.

"Thanks, Ms. Bowley," Violet said.

The librarian checked out the books.

"You're welcome," she said. "And remember, no more climbing on shelves!"

"Okay!" Violet said. She ran out of the library. Sprite flew behind her until he caught up. Then he settled on her shoulder.

"What do we do with these?" Sprite asked. "Jolt said he'd never read a book."

"I don't think Jolt knows how good books are," Violet said. "I can read them to him. He'll probably like them so much that he'll put down his video game."

"It's worth a try," Sprite said. "Let's go home."

Violet and Sprite walked behind a tree. Sprite took out some pixie dust. Violet held the books tightly. She didn't want them to get lost during the trip.

Before Sprite could throw the dust, Violet gasped.

One of the books in her hands was floating in the air.

Then it flew away!

Chapter Seven
Another Pixie?

"Sprite!" Violet cried. "What's happening?"

"I'm not sure," Sprite said.

The book flew high in the sky. Then it landed on the roof of the library.

"No!" yelled Violet.

Then the second book began to float.

Violet tried to grab it.

But that book flew away, too.

Violet ran after the book.

Then she saw something.

Pixie dust!

"Sprite!" she said. "Pixie dust is making the books fly away."

"It's not me!" Sprite said. "It must be another pixie. One trying to stop us."

"We have to do something!" Violet said.

Sprite took out his Royal Pixie Tricker medal.

"By order of Queen Mab," he said, "show yourself!"

The second book flew up in the sky. It landed on a high tree branch.

But there was no pixie in sight.

Violet felt the third book twitch in her hands. She held on tightly.

"Can't we stop it?" Violet asked.

"Not unless we know who it is," Sprite said.

Then Violet and Sprite heard a giggle. It came from the tree.

Violet looked. She saw a flash of yellow.

"Who are you?" she asked.

Another giggle.

"Never mind, Violet," Sprite said in a loud voice. "It's obvious. This pixie is too scared to face me."

"Hey!" came a voice.

A small fairy popped out from behind the tree. She was dressed in a yellow striped shirt and overalls.

"Spoiler!" Sprite cried.

"Get real, Sprite," Spoiler said. "I'm not afraid of you."

Sprite puffed out his chest. "Well, maybe you should be. I am a Royal Pixie Tricker."

Spoiler rolled her eyes. "Please. You couldn't trick yourself!"

Sprite flew up to Violet's ear. He whispered, "Say Spoiler's name backwards three times. It's small magic. But it should work for now."

Violet nodded. She had done this before.

"So what are you gonna do, Sprite?" Spoiler said. "Ooh, I'm so scared."

Violet took a deep breath.

"Reliops, Reliops, Reliops!" she shouted.

Spoiler frowned. "Rats!" she said.

In a flash, Spoiler vanished.

"Is she gone for good?" Violet asked.

Sprite shook his head. "No. To send her back to the Otherworld, we have to trick her. But that should keep her away for a little bit."

"Good," Violet said.

"Should I fly up and get those books?" Sprite asked.

"Do it fast," Violet said. "We have to go save Leon!"

Chapter Eight
Jolt Escapes

After Sprite had rescued the other books, it was time to save Leon. Sprite threw some pixie dust on Violet.

"Achoo!" She forgot to hold her nose.

The library vanished. They were back in Leon's room.

Jolt was still playing the video game. His eyes looked glazed.

"Almost there," Jolt said.

Violet looked at the screen. It said LEVEL 9. The picture looked like a desert. Leon was walking down a sandy trail.

"Leon's still okay," Violet said. "We made it just in time."

"This level doesn't look so bad," Sprite said. "Not as bad as those rocks."

Jolt grinned. "Just wait!" He moved the joystick, and Leon walked to a hole in the desert sand.

A big snake popped up. It hissed in Leon's face.

"Aaaaaaah!" Leon yelled.

"I remember this level," Violet said. "You have to go through the desert without getting bitten by a snake."

"Hee-hee-hee," Jolt laughed. Then he paused the game.

"So what are you guys doing?" he asked. "Do you think you can get me to read a book?"

"No," Violet lied. "I'm just going to sit here and read a book I got."

Jolt hit the play button. "Fine with me. I'll just keep playing the game."

Violet sat on the floor. She opened up one of the books. It was *Peter Pan.*

Violet began to read aloud. From time to time, Sprite nudged her.

"It's not exciting enough," Sprite said. "Get to a good part."

Violet read as quickly as she could. Jolt ignored her. He kept playing the game.

Violet looked up at the screen. Now Leon was in level ten. It was a jungle filled with pits of quicksand. Leon had to avoid the pits.

This has got to work, Violet thought. Jolt might lose the game at level eleven. And then what will happen to Leon?

Violet read faster. She told the story of Peter Pan. How he brought Wendy, Michael, and John to Neverland. And a band of pirates caught them. The pirates were led by Captain Hook.

Soon Violet got near the end of the story. She looked at Jolt. The gremlin had paused the game. He was pretending to play. But he was really listening to Violet.

"It's working! It's working!" Sprite whispered in Violet's ear.

Violet nodded. She got to the part when Peter Pan and Hook had their final fight.

"'Suddenly, the sword fell from Hook's hand,'" Violet read, "'and he was at Peter's mercy.'"

Then Violet stopped.

"Well, that's it," she said, closing the book.

Jolt stood up. "What do you mean that's it?" he asked. "What happened to Hook?"

Violet shrugged. "I don't know," she said. "That's all there is."

"It can't be!" Jolt said.

Jolt hopped off the bed. He grabbed the book from Violet's hands.

"Let me see that!" he said.

Violet and Sprite smiled at each other.

Violet's plan was working!

"If Jolt reads the book, he'll be tricked," Sprite whispered. "Then his magic will be broken."

Violet and Sprite waited for Jolt to open the book.

Jolt stopped.

He put down the book.

"Ha!" he said. "You can't trick me that easily."

"Oh, no," Violet moaned.

Jolt hopped back onto the bed. He picked up the controls. Then he hit the play button.

Jolt opened his hand. It was filled with pixie dust.

"See ya!" Jolt said.

Jolt sprinkled the pixie dust over his head. He disappeared.

"Where did he go?" Violet asked.

Sprite pointed at the screen. "Look," he said.

Jolt was in the video game with Leon!

Chapter Nine
Inside the Game

"There's only one thing to do now," Sprite said.

"Uh, tell Aunt Anne that Leon ran away?" Violet asked hopefully. But she knew what Sprite was thinking.

Sprite took out some pixie dust. "We have to follow them into the game!"

"I know," Violet said. She held her nose and closed her eyes.

Sprite sprinkled the pixie dust on them. Violet opened her eyes.

She felt weird. Like she was flat.

Violet looked around. Green jungle plants were everywhere. Big, bright flowers grew as tall as she was.

Sprite had done it. They were in the video game!

In the distance, Violet saw Leon running away. Jolt was behind him.

"Over there!" Violet said.

She started to run through the jungle. Sprite flew next to her.

"Violet," Sprite said, "don't forget about the —"

"Aaaaaaaah!" Violet yelled. Her right foot stepped in something soft.

"Quicksand!" Sprite said.

"Help!" Violet said. The quicksand was sticky. It felt alive. It felt like it was grabbing her foot. Now her whole leg was in the quicksand. She was sinking!

"Oh, no! I'll think of something," Sprite said.

Sprite flew around Violet. He still had some pixie dust in his hand.

Sprite sprinkled the pixie dust on a vine. The vine crawled toward Violet. It wrapped around Violet's waist.

"This is even scarier than the quicksand!" Violet said.

"Just wait," Sprite said.

The vine pulled Violet out of the pit. Then it dropped Violet onto the jungle floor.

Violet stood up. "Thanks," she said. "Now let's go!"

Violet ran through the jungle. This time, she kept her eyes on the ground. If she saw quicksand, she ran around it.

Soon they had almost caught up with Leon and Jolt.

"Leon!" Violet said. "It's me!"

Leon turned around. The look of fear left his face. Now he looked confused.

"Violet?" he asked. "How did you get in here?"

Jolt smiled. "No time for reunions. Time for level eleven!"

Jolt hit a button on the controls.

What kind of game is this? Violet thought. Where will we end up now?

The jungle faded. Now tall redbrick walls surrounded them. They were in some kind of hallway.

"What's this?" Violet asked.

"Level eleven," Jolt said. "It's a maze. I've never made it to the end before. But now that I'm in the game, I can't lose!"

Jolt ran down the hall. He made a left turn.

"Violet, what's going on?" Leon asked. "And who's the guy with the wings?"

Sprite frowned.

"It's just a dream, Leon," Violet said. "You're dreaming that we're trapped in the video game."

"Okay," Leon said. But he didn't sound like he believed her.

"And now we have to catch that guy who just ran away," Violet said. She ran down the hallway.

Leon ran after her. "But that's not part of the game!" he said.

"It is now," Violet said. "Hurry up! Follow that gremlin!"

She made a left turn. There was another hallway. Jolt was nowhere in sight.

Leon stepped in front of her.

"You're no good at this," he said. "I've played up to this level before. You should follow me."

Violet wanted to argue. But she knew Leon was right.

So Violet and Sprite followed Leon. They made turn after turn after turn. But there was no sign of Jolt.

Then they heard a voice.

"Drat!"

It was Jolt.

"Double drat!" Jolt cried.

"Over here," Leon said. He made a right turn. Violet and Sprite followed.

Jolt was at a dead end. There was nowhere to turn.

"I hate this maze!" Jolt said. "I've never made it out yet."

Jolt pounded his fists against the wall. Then he kicked the wall with his boot.

"Stupid, stupid game!" he yelled.

Leon reached into his shirt pocket. He pulled out a book.

Action Kingdom Guide.

"Don't go crazy, dude," Leon said. "Take a look at this. It will tell you how to get out."

Leon tossed the guide to Jolt.

Jolt flipped through the guide.

"Let's see," he muttered. "Level eleven. Ah, here it is."

Then Jolt started to read from the book.

Chapter Ten
Leon Saves the Day

"'To get through the maze, you should — '"
Jolt began.

Then he stopped.

A strange wind started to whip around the gremlin.

"Oh, no," he said. "It's not fair! This is a guide, not a book!"

"Looks like a book to me," said Sprite with a giggle.

The wind formed a large funnel in the air. The whirling wind pulled Jolt into the funnel.

"But I don't know how the game ends!" Jolt cried.

Jolt vanished inside the funnel. The wind suddenly stopped.

Then a bright light flashed.

Violet didn't feel flat anymore. She

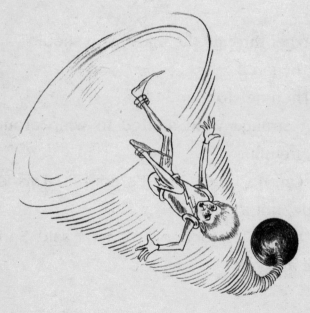

looked around. She was back in Leon's room. Leon was there, too. So was Sprite.

"Did it work?" Violet asked Sprite. "Did we really trick him?"

Sprite took out the *Book of Tricks.* He turned to the page where Jolt's picture should be. Then he flew up near Violet's face so she could see.

The page used to be blank. But a faint picture was forming. The picture got darker in front of Violet's eyes. Soon Jolt's picture filled the page.

"That means we did it!" Violet said. "We tricked Jolt. Everything is back to normal."

"Uh, almost," Sprite said.

Violet turned around. Leon stood with his arms folded across his chest. He looked angry.

"This is not a dream," he said.

"No," Violet said.

"Who's the bug?" Leon asked. He nodded his head toward Sprite.

Sprite flew in front of Leon's face. "I'm not a bug!" he said. "I'm a Royal Pixie Tricker."

Violet tried to back out the door. "Couldn't you just forget this happened?" she asked Leon.

"No way," Leon said. "I almost got flattened by boulders. And bitten by snakes. And drowned in quicksand. I can't forget that."

"I guess not," Violet said.

"Besides," Leon said. "If it wasn't for me, we'd still be in that game. That gremlin guy didn't go away until I gave him that book."

Violet didn't know what to do. Leon was right. But could she trust him? She wasn't sure.

"I can't tell you what's happening," she said. "I just can't."

"Tell me everything," Leon said firmly. "Or I'll tell my mom. Yours, too."

Violet looked at Sprite. Sprite shrugged.

"Okay, I'll tell you," she said.

Violet sat down on the floor. So much was happening!

Jolt was back in the Otherworld. That made two fairies tricked. Twelve to go.

But now Violet had to tell Leon the whole story.

Would Leon keep their secret?

Would they trick the rest of the fairies?

Sprite knew what Violet was thinking.

"Don't worry, Violet," he whispered in her ear. "We'll just have to wait and see what happens next!"

Pixie Tricks Stickers

Use the stickers with your *Book of Tricks.* When Sprite and Violet catch a pixie, stick the sticker in the book.
(Pixie Secret: Some of these pixies haven't been caught yet. Save the stickers to use later.)

·Pixie·Tricks·

_____'s

(YOUR NAME)

Book of Tricks

Sprite has his Book of Tricks.

Now you have your very own, too!

Use this book each time Violet and Sprite
catch a pixie. Here's what you do:

1. Put the pixie's sticker next to its name.

2. Write when Sprite and Violet sent the
pixie back to the Otherworld.

3. Write the magic rhyme from Sprite's Book
of Tricks. It tells how to trick the pixie.

4. One sticker shows something the pixie
put a spell on. Put that sticker in the book.
For example, Pix put a spell on a dodgeball
in the first book, so you would put the
dodgeball sticker on Pix's page.

5. One sticker shows what Violet and Sprite used to trick the pixie. Put that sticker in the book, too. For example, Violet and Sprite used a seesaw to trick Pix in the first book, so you would put the seesaw on Pix's page.

Hint 1: You might not have all the stickers you need at first. Look for the other stickers you need in later Pixie Tricks adventures!

Hint 2: Read the labels next to the stickers on the sticker page. These labels will help you figure out where each sticker should go.

When you've collected all the stickers and filled in this book, you'll be a Royal Pixie Tricker. Just like Sprite.

Good luck!

The Poem
from the Fairy
Queen's Book

If ever pixies do escape

Through the old oak tree,

Here is what you have to do

Or trouble there will be.

First find a Pixie Tricker,

The youngest in the land.

Send him to the human world,

The *Book of Tricks* in hand.

Once he's there he'll find a girl

Who's only eight years old.

But she's a smart and clever girl

Who's also very bold.

He must ask her for her help

And if she does agree,

They'll trick the pixies, one by one

Till no more do they see.

Only they can do the job.

It's much more than a game.

For if they fail to trick them all

The world won't be the same!

How to Find an Escaped Pixie

Tracking down pixies can be tricky. You could search and search and never find one. Or one could pop up in front of your nose when you least expect it! You never know what a pixie will do!

People have all kinds of ideas about how to find pixies.

● Some people look at dawn and sundown, or at noon and midnight. Pixies like the in-between times, when it's not quite morning or afternoon, and neither day nor night.

- A ring of mushrooms growing out of the ground could be a sign of a pixie ring.

- Pixies love wild places in nature. Look in woods, meadows, and around mountains.

- Pixies often gather where two points meet. Where the ocean meets the sand or where one road meets another are good places to see pixies.

- Pixies love flowers and trees. That butterfly you've seen flitting around your garden might be a pixie in disguise!

How to Trick a Pixie

You now know where to look for a pixie. But what should you do when you find it?

To send an escaped pixie back to the Otherworld, you have to trick it. The best way to trick a pixie is to get it to do something different than it usually does. For example, to trick a pixie that always lies, you would have to get it to tell the truth.

Here are some famous pixies who once escaped into the human world. A Royal Pixie Tricker tricked them and they were sent back. Can you figure out how they were tricked? Take this quiz to find out.

Weepy was a gnome who cried all the time.

How do you think Weepy was tricked? _____

_____

Zzzeke was an elf who slept late every morning.

How do you think Zzzeke was tricked? _____

_____

Cavity was a troll who never brushed his teeth.

How do you think Cavity was tricked? _____

_____

Turn the page upside down for the answers.

How did you do? If you got all three right, you're ready to start tricking pixies!

Sprite

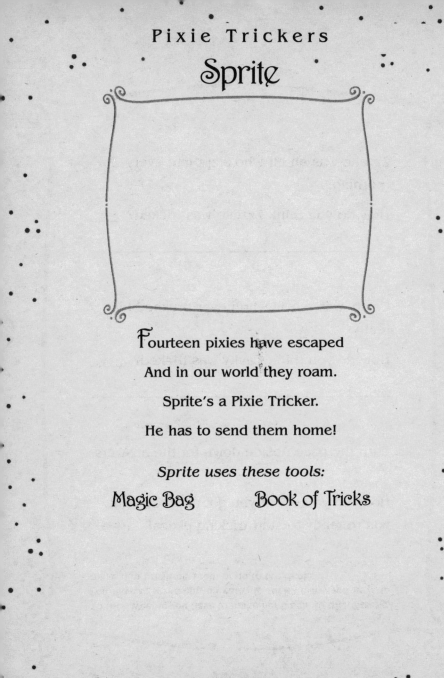

Fourteen pixies have escaped

And in our world they roam.

Sprite's a Pixie Tricker.

He has to send them home!

Sprite uses these tools:

Magic Bag   Book of Tricks

Pixie Trickers
Violet

Sprite will need to find some help,

Someone who's smart and bold.

He will ask a little girl,

Who's only eight years old.

She must give Sprite her word.

She'll help him take a stand.

Then they'll trick the pixies

And return them to their land.

Aquamarina

Aquamarina has a flair

For making faucets run.

She's causing leaks all over town

And thinks it's lots of fun!

Caught in book #: _____

Magic rhyme: _____

_____

Aquamarina put a spell on this: The Pixie Trickers used
                                      this to trick Aquamarina:

Bogey Bill

Creepy critters, slimy snakes,

A really scary dream.

This freaky goblin will try it all

Just to hear you scream.

Caught in book #: _____

Magic rhyme: _____

_____

Bogey Bill put a spell on this:

The Pixie Trickers used
this to trick Bogey Bill:

Buttercup

Ħiccups in the morning, hiccups in the night.

If you've got the hiccups, then Buttercup's in sight.

Caught in book #: _____

Magic rhyme: _____

_____

Buttercup put a spell on this: The Pixie Trickers used
                                        this to trick Buttercup:

Fixit

Here's a special warning
To all you girls and boys:
Fixit can be nasty
When making all your toys!

Caught in book #: _____

Magic rhyme: _____

_____

Fixit put a spell on this: The Pixie Trickers used
                                             this to trick Fixit:

Escaped Pixies
Greenie and Meanie

Watch out for your pets, with these two dwarves around.

They'll take them far away, where pets cannot be found.

Caught in book #: _____ .

Magic rhyme: _____

_____

Greenie and Meanie
put a spell on this:

The Pixie Trickers used this
to trick Greenie and Meanie:

Hinky Pink

If it's raining when the sun is out,

Then Hinky Pink is near.

He can make it rain or snow,

And then he'll disappear.

Caught in book #: _____

Magic rhyme: _____

_____

Hinky Pink put a spell on this: The Pixie Trickers used
                                         this to trick Hinky Pink:

Jolt

Jolt likes a gadget,

Jolt loves a game.

But once he gets a hold of it,

It will not be the same.

Caught in book #: _____

Magic rhyme: _____

_____

Jolt put a spell on this:

The Pixie Trickers used
this to trick Jolt:

Escaped Pixies
Pix

No more homework, no more chores,

Everyone must play.

That's the way the world would be

If Pix had things his way.

Caught in book #: _____

Magic rhyme: _____

_____

Pix put a spell on this: The Pixie Trickers used
this to trick Pix:

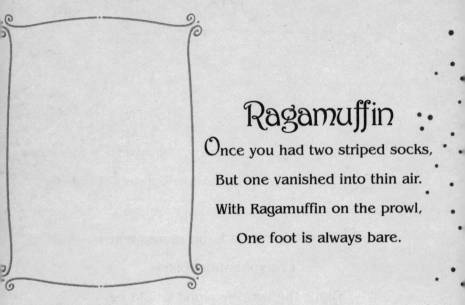

Ragamuffin

Once you had two striped socks,

But one vanished into thin air.

With Ragamuffin on the prowl,

One foot is always bare.

Caught in book #: _____

Magic rhyme: _____

_____

Ragamuffin put a spell on this: The Pixie Trickers used
                                   this to trick Ragamuffin:

Rusella

If there are mixed-up messages
And everything's confused,
Rusella might be playing games.
That's how she stays amused.

Caught in book #: _____

Magic rhyme: _____

_____

Rusella put a spell on this: The Pixie Trickers used
                                      this to trick Rusella:

Spoiler

When everything seems perfect,

When everything seems right,

You can sure bet Spoiler,

Will wreck it all for spite.

Caught in book #: _____

Magic rhyme: _____

_____

Spoiler put a spell on this: The Pixie Trickers used
                                      this to trick Spoiler:

Sport

No shots, no goals, no points,

You just can't win the game?

If the rules just don't seem fair,

Maybe Sport's to blame!

Caught in book #: _____

Magic rhyme: _____

_____

Sport put a spell on this: The Pixie Trickers used
                                  this to trick Sport:

Finn

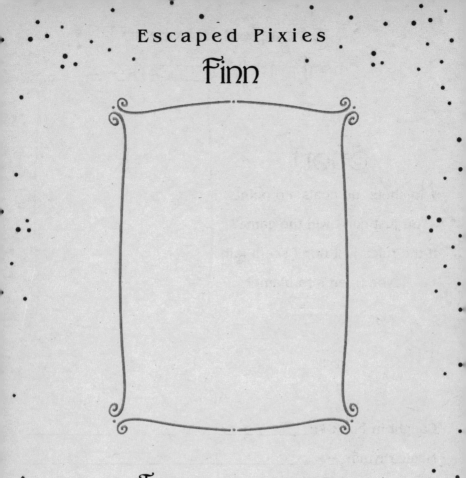

There is a big, bad wizard

With an evil, nasty grin.

He helped the pixies all escape.

His name is Wizard Finn.

First seen in book #: _____

A Friend Indeed
Robert B. Gnome

Robert lives in the human world,

Where he's a garden gnome.

He'll help the Trickers find out how

To send the pixies home.

First seen in book #: _____

The Fairy Queen
Queen Mab

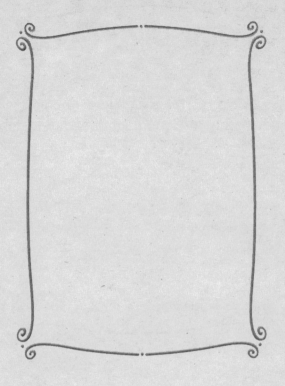

Queen Mab protects the Otherworld.

She's brave and wise and nice.

She helps trick the pixies

By sharing sage advice.

The Pixie Code

It's not easy to track a pixie. If you are working with a friend, you might need to keep your messages secret.

Use the code wheel on the next page to keep your messages safe from prying pixie eyes. Here's how it works:

1. Write your message:

   I HAVE FOUND THE PIXIE.

2. Start with the first letter. Find the letter on the outside wheel. Then see what letter it matches up with on the inside wheel. That is your code letter: I = A

3. Write the rest of your message using the code wheel:

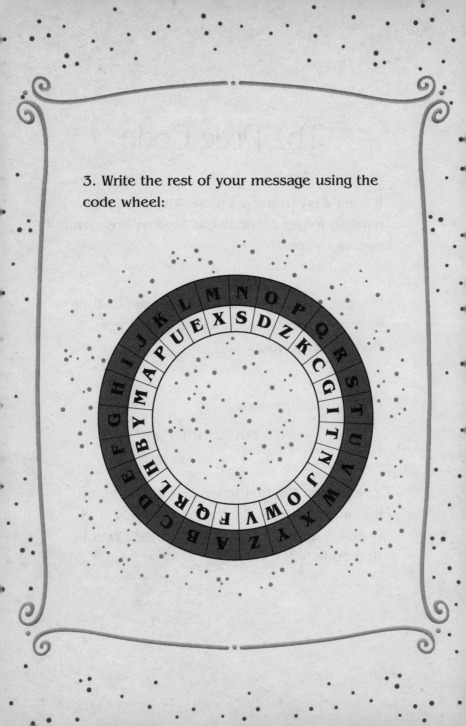

4. Give a copy of the code wheel to your friend. Tell your friend to look up each letter on the inside of the wheel and match it to the letter on the outside of the wheel. Then your friend can decode the message:

A MFNH BDTSL IMH ZAOAH.

I HAVE FOUND THE PIXIE.

Your Page

Your name: _____

Age: _____

Favorite Pixie Tricker: _____

Favorite escaped pixie: _____

Favorite Pixie Tricks book: _____

If you could invent a magic tool to help

Sprite and Violet, what would it be? _____

_____

Congratulations!

I HEREBY GIVE

_____

(Your name here)

THE TITLE OF Royal Pixie Tricker

FOR TRICKING ALL FOURTEEN PIXIES

AND SENDING THEM BACK

TO THE OTHERWORLD.

The next time you're out walking

On a bright and sunny day,

Remember all you've read

About the pixie way.

Keep your eyes wide open,

And take your steps with care.

For if you're very lucky,

You might see a pixie there.